# Hugh Lofting's
# Travels of
# Doctor Dolittle

THIS BOOK BELONGS TO

Mark Rankin

Ardwreck School

ADAPTED FOR BEGINNING READERS

By Al Perkins / Illustrated by Philip Wende

**COLLINS**

Below is a list of the original Doctor Dolittle books written
by Hugh Lofting and published by Jonathan Cape Ltd.

THE STORY OF DOCTOR DOLITTLE
THE VOYAGES OF DOCTOR DOLITTLE
DOCTOR DOLITTLE'S POST OFFICE
DOCTOR DOLITTLE'S CIRCUS
DOCTOR DOLITTLE'S ZOO
DOCTOR DOLITTLE'S CARAVAN
DOCTOR DOLITTLE'S GARDEN
DOCTOR DOLITTLE IN THE MOON
DOCTOR DOLITTLE'S RETURN
DOCTOR DOLITTLE AND THE SECRET LAKE
DOCTOR DOLITTLE AND THE GREEN CANARY
DOCTOR DOLITTLE'S PUDDLEBY ADVENTURES

4 5 6 7 8 9 10

ISBN 0 00 171328 0 (paperback)
ISBN 0 00 171130 X (hardback)

© Copyright 1967, by Bernard M. Silbert,
Executor of the estate of Josephine Lofting
From 'The story of Doctor Dolittle' by Hugh Lofting
A Beginner Book published by arrangement with
Random House, Inc., New York, New York
First published in Great Britain 1968

Printed in Great Britain by
William Collins Sons & Co Ltd, Glasgow

Once upon a time, there was a doctor named

JOHN
DOLITTLE
M.D.

The M.D. meant that he was a doctor
and that he knew a lot.

Doctor Dolittle lived in a
little town in England called
Puddleby-on-the-Marsh.

PUDDLEBY
ON THE
MARSH

When he walked down the street in his
high hat, all the dogs and cats and cows
and horses and pigs and chickens and
sheep and frogs and turtles ran after him.

Instead of doctoring people, Doctor Dolittle
doctored animals. He was very fond of
animals. And animals were very fond of him.
They came to his house from everywhere so
that he could take care of them. Then,
instead of going home again, they stayed.

Soon his house was filled with all kinds
of animals. There was barely enough room
left for Doctor Dolittle himself.

Doctor Dolittle gave names to some of his favourite pets:

There was Dab-Dab the duck

And Jip the dog

And Gub-Gub the pig

8

Too-Too the owl

And Polynesia the parrot.

But the Doctor had so many mice and canaries and hens and roosters and turtles and rabbits and hedgehogs and alligators and opossums and raccoons that he couldn't find names for them all.

One rainy day, Polynesia the parrot
said to Doctor Dolittle, "You have so
many pets now that you must learn
to talk with them. We will teach you
animal language."

Doctor Dolittle sat down in front of a blackboard. His pets gave him lessons. Soon he learned to talk with the animals. Soon he understood everything they said.

11

One night, after the Doctor had learned
the animal language, the door flew open.
A monkey ran in.

"Doctor!" the monkey cried.

"My name is Chee-Chee.

"I have come all the way from Africa
to tell you about the monkeys.
They have a terrible sickness.
They beg you to come to Africa to cure
them. Will you do it, *please?*"

"Of course I will," said Doctor Dolittle.
So, early next morning, the Doctor and
Chee-Chee and Jip and Dab-Dab and
Gub-Gub and Too-Too and Polynesia took
all their luggage down to the seashore.

Doctor Dolittle got a boat from a sailor.
Then they all went on board.

15

For six weeks, they sailed
on and on,
over the
rolling sea.

When they got to the Equator,
they saw some flying fishes.

The flying fishes said,

"It is only 50 miles to Africa."

But then a great storm came up
with thunder and lightning.
The wind howled.
The rain poured down.

The waves splashed over the boat.

Suddenly, there was a big *"Boom!"*

The ship stopped.

It rolled over on its side.

"Dear me," said the Doctor.

"We must have run into Africa." 19

"Get the rope." cried Polynesia.

"Dab-Dab, you take the end of the rope.

Fly to the shore.

Tie it to a palm tree.

"Then those who can't swim go down
the rope until you get to the land."
And that's how they all got safely
to the shore.

They all took shelter in a nice dry cave
they found up in the cliffs.

Suddenly Chee-Chee said, "Shhhhhhh!
I hear footsteps."

They looked out and saw
a soldier come out of the woods.
He wore a mask over his face.
He carried a shield and
a long, sharp spear.

"You must all come before the Great King
of the Jolliginki," he said.

"All these lands belong to him.

Follow me!"

When they had followed the soldier
a little way through the forest,
they saw the King's palace. The King
was sitting under an umbrella.
"You may not travel through my lands,"
said the King.
Then he told his soldiers,
"Take this medicine-man away!
Lock him and all his animals
in my strongest prison!"

27

The prison had only one little window.
It was high up in the wall, with bars
across it. The prison door was strong
and thick. The walls were solid stone.
Gub-Gub the pig began to cry.
Even Doctor Dolittle looked worried.

But Polynesia the parrot said,
"I'm small enough to get through the
bars of this window. Tonight I'll creep
through the bars and fly to the palace.
I'll find a way to make the King
let you out."

So that night the parrot flew to the palace. She crept into the King's bedroom very softly and hid under the bed. "I am Doctor Dolittle," said the parrot, just the way the Doctor would have said it. "You cannot see me. I have made myself invisible. Now listen! I warn you!

"You let me and my animals travel
through your kingdom, or I will make
you sick like the monkeys. Send your
soldiers to open the prison door,
or you shall have *mumps* before
the morning sun comes up."

At those words, the King began
to tremble. He jumped out of bed.

He told the soldiers to open the
prison door. The Doctor and all
his animals rushed out of the prison.

They ran through the forest
toward the land of the monkeys.
They ran as fast as they could.

But when the King found out how he
had been fooled by the parrot, he
was dreadfully angry. He rushed around
in his night-shirt. He woke up all his
army. He sent them into the jungle
to catch the Doctor.

Chee-Chee the monkey knew the paths
through the jungle better than
the King's soldiers did. He led
the Doctor and his pets to
the thickest part of the forest.

He hid them all in a big hollow tree. Chee-Chee said, "We must hide here while the soldiers are close by. Soon they will get tired and go back to bed."

When the soldiers had all gone,
Chee-Chee brought the Doctor and his
animals out of their hiding place.
Then they set off for the Land
of the Monkeys.

And that very evening, they saw a lot
of monkeys. They were sitting in the
trees, looking and eagerly waiting.
When they saw the famous Doctor, the
monkeys made a tremendous noise.
They cheered. They waved.
They swung out on branches to greet him.

But the King's soldiers hadn't gone
to bed. They were still following.
They saw Doctor Dolittle.
They ran to catch him.
The Doctor and his animals ran harder
than they had ever run in their lives.

They came to a high place
with a river far below it.
The Land of the Monkeys was
on the other side.

Jip the dog
looked over the edge
and almost fell.
"How are we ever
going to get across?"
he asked.

Then the leader of the monkeys,
the biggest one of all, cried out
to the others, "Boys! A bridge!
Quick! Get lively!
Make a bridge! A bridge!"
And, quick as a flash . . .
. . . the monkeys made themselves
into a bridge. They did it by holding
40  hands, and feet, and tails.

They made a bridge of monkeys.
And the big one shouted, "Walk over!
All of you! Walk across our bridge!"

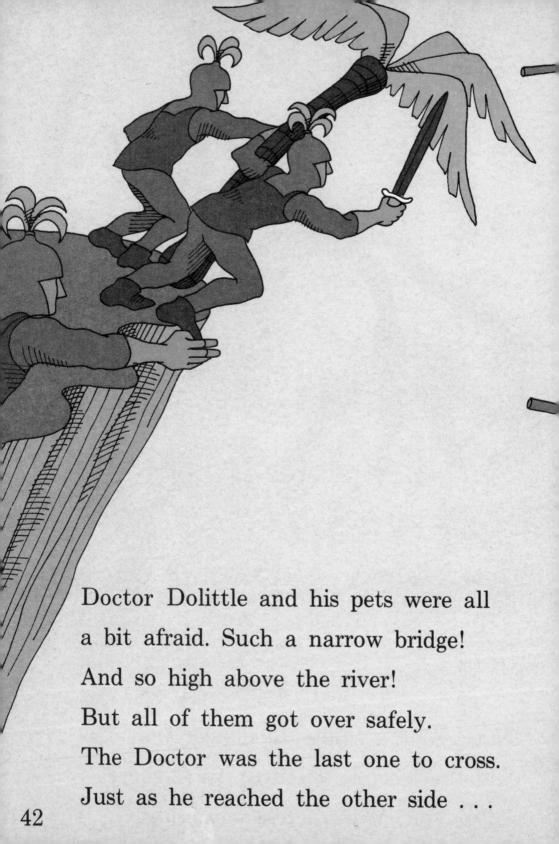

Doctor Dolittle and his pets were all
a bit afraid. Such a narrow bridge!
And so high above the river!
But all of them got over safely.
The Doctor was the last one to cross.
Just as he reached the other side . . .

. . . the King's soldiers came
rushing up behind them. They waved
their swords. They threw their spears.
They howled and they yowled.
But they were too late.
Doctor Dolittle and all his animals
were safe in the Land of the Monkeys.

The Doctor found hundreds and thousands
of very sick monkeys. He made all
the monkeys come to be vaccinated.
For three days and three nights
they came from the jungles.
They came from the valleys.
They came from the mountains and hills.

They came to a little house of grass,
where the Doctor sat all day and all night,
vaccinating, vaccinating and vaccinating.
And then, very soon, the monkeys
began to get better.

By then, the Doctor was all worn out.
He was so tired that he went to bed
and slept for three days and three nights
without even turning over.

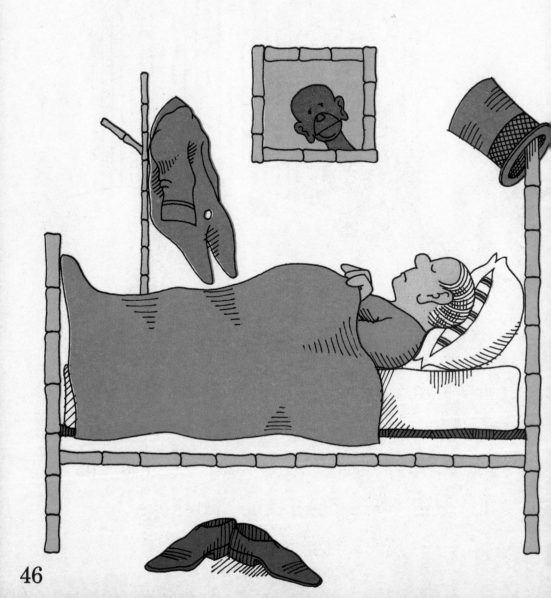

When he woke up, Doctor Dolittle saw
that none of the monkeys were sick
any more. They were all well!
His vaccinations had cured them all.
So he told them that now he must
go back home to Puddleby-on-the-Marsh.

The monkeys were very surprised at this.
They had hoped that the Doctor
would stay with them forever.
That night they got together to talk
things over. The big one got up and said,
"It is sad that Doctor Dolittle must
leave us. But since he must go,
let us give him a fine present."

"If you *really* want to please him,"
Chee-Chee said, "give him an animal—
one he has never seen before."
"An iguana?"
"No!"
"An okapi?"
"No!"
"A pushmi-pullyu?"
*"Yes!"*
"No man has ever seen a pushmi-pullyu.
Let us give him a pushmi-pullyu."

48

Now there aren't any pushmi-pullyus any
more. But then, when Doctor Dolittle
was in Africa, there were still
a few of them left.
The pushmi-pullyu had no tail.
Instead, he had a head, with horns,
both in front and behind.

Pushmi-pullyus, with their two heads,
were very hard to catch.
When one head went to sleep,
the other head was always wide awake
and watching. This is why they were
never caught and never seen in zoos.

To catch a pushmi-pullyu for the Doctor
the monkeys made a plan.
Very, very quietly, they set out
through the forest to hunt.

They found a place where they thought
the pushmi-pullyu might be.

Then they made a circle and joined hands.
The pushmi-pullyu heard them.
He tried to break through the ring
of monkeys. But he couldn't do it!

He saw it was no use. He sat down
and asked them what they wanted.
They asked him if he would go home
with Doctor Dolittle.

The pushmi-pullyu shook his heads hard.
"Certainly not!" he said.
For three days and three nights
the monkeys tried to persuade him.
Then at last he said, "I will come
with you and see what kind of man
this Doctor is."

The pushmi-pullyu took one look
at Doctor Dolittle. He saw at once
that the Doctor was a very good man.
The pushmi-pullyu said, "You have been
most kind to all these monkeys.
I have made up my mind.
I will go with you."

Then the Doctor, the Doctor's animals
and the pushmi-pullyu started back
to the seashore. The monkeys
went with them to see them off.

It took a long time to say "Farewell!"
Hundreds and thousands of monkeys
wanted to shake the Doctor by the
hand and thank him for making them
well again.

Then the pushmi-pullyu,
Gub-Gub, Dab-Dab, Jip, Too-Too,
Polynesia and Chee-Chee
all went on the ship with the Doctor.

Soon they were out of sight of land.
The wide, wide sea looked terribly big
and lonesome. They lost their way.
They had no more food. There was no
wind to fill the sail. Doctor Dolittle
said, "I am afraid we are never going
to get home." But then they heard
a strange noise high in the air.
It grew louder and *louder* and LOUDER.

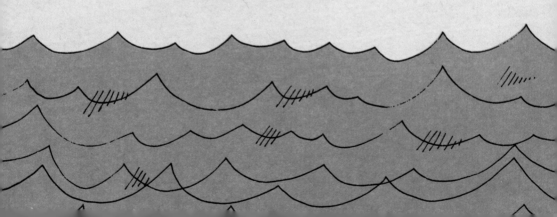

Birds!

Millions of them! Millions of swallows,
flying fast. The swallows saw the ship.

They came down close. They swooped
and skimmed over the water.
They took hold of ropes with their feet.
Away they flew. They pulled the ship
along behind them!

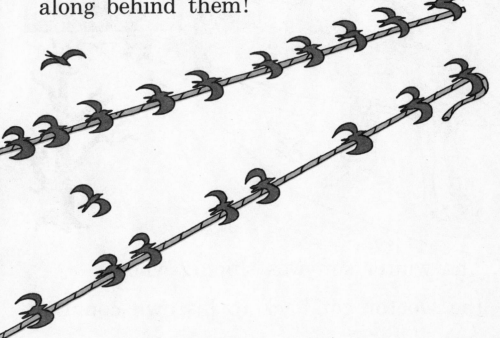

Now the Doctor was travelling fast.
He had to hold on to his hat
with both hands.
The swallows flew on and on.
They pulled and pulled.
They pulled the ship to England
in almost no time at all.

The winter sun was shining when
the Doctor got back to his own country.
It was good to be home at last.
Every night after supper the Doctor and
his animals would sit around the big,
warm fire. Then the Doctor would read
aloud to them. He would read them the
big book he was writing about their trip
to faraway Africa.

Africa! The land they would never
forget! The land where the monkeys
chattered in the palm trees.
The land where they found the
wonderful pushmi-pullyu!

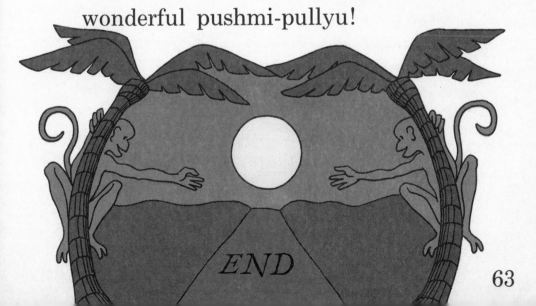

*END*